The Granny Game

Beverly Lewis

Beverly Lewis Books for Young Readers

PICTURE BOOKS

Annika's Secret Wish
Cows in the House
Just Like Mama
What Is Heaven Like?

THE CUL-DE-SAC KIDS

The Double Dabble Surprise
The Chicken Pox Panic
The Crazy Christmas Angel Mystery
No Grown-ups Allowed
Frog Power
The Mystery of Case D. Luc
The Stinky Sneakers Mystery
Pickle Pizza
Mailbox Mania
The Mudhole Mystery
Fiddlesticks
The Crabby Cat Caper
Tarantula Toes
Green Gravy
Backyard Bandit Mystery
Tree House Trouble
The Creepy Sleep-Over
The Great TV Turn-Off
Piggy Party
The Granny Game
Mystery Mutt
Big Bad Beans
The Upside-Down Day
The Midnight Mystery

Katie and Jake and the Haircut Mistake

www.BeverlyLewis.com

06C

THE CUL-DE-SAC KIDS

The Granny
Game

Beverly Lewis

BETHANY HOUSE PUBLISHERS
MINNEAPOLIS, MINNESOTA 55438

The Granny Game
Copyright © 1999
Beverly Lewis

Cover illustration by Paul Turnbaugh
Text illustrations by Janet Huntington
Cover design by Lookout Design Group

Published by Bethany House Publishers
11400 Hampshire Avenue South
Bloomington, Minnesota 55438

Bethany House Publishers is a division of
Baker Publishing Group, Grand Rapids, Michigan.

Printed in the United States of America

ISBN-13: 978-0-7642-2125-5
ISBN-10: 0-7642-2125-6

Library of Congress Cataloging-in-Publication Data
Lewis, Beverly, 1949–
    The granny game / by Beverly Lewis.
        p.   cm. — (The cul-de-sac kids ; 20)
    ISBN 0-7642-2125-6 (pbk.)
[1. Grandmothers—Fiction. 2. Brothers and sisters—
Fiction. 3. Christian life—Fiction.] I. Title.
    PZ7.L58464   Got   1999
    [Fic]—dc21

                                              00-504217

To
Carol Johnson,

a fun-loving grandma,
who enjoys both broccoli
and chocolate cake.

THE CUL-DE-SAC KIDS

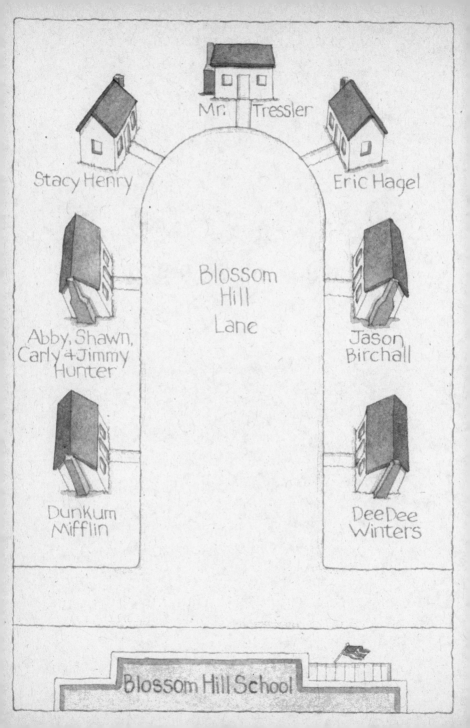

ONE

Abby Hunter felt like a jitterbox.

Grandma Hunter was coming for the weekend. The pickiest grandma in the west.

Abby dusted and mopped. She checked under the guest room bed. She looked behind the dresser.

Everything must be spotless and neat.

Abby stepped back for a final look. "Double dabble good," she said.

Mother came in just then. "Thank you for helping, Abby. What a nice, clean room," she said.

"Will Grandma notice?" Abby asked. She really hoped so.

Her mother nodded. "Only one thing is missing," she said with a smile. "Can you guess?"

Abby looked all around the room. "Flowers! Grandma likes fresh flowers," she said.

"You're right." Mother gave Abby a big hug. "We'll buy some at the florist."

She looked up at her mother. "I'm going to miss you and Daddy while you're gone."

"We'll miss you, too, honey. But Grandma will take good care of you. And your sister and brothers." Mother kissed the top of Abby's head. "The weekend will go fast."

Suddenly, Abby remembered something about Grandma's cooking.

Her stomach churned.

Her taste buds faded.

Her nose twitched.

Grandma's favorite foods were yucky. She liked to cook things like broccoli, Brus-

11

sels sprouts, and asparagus. The greenest, smelliest vegetables in the world!

Quickly, she told her mother, "Carly and Jimmy will make a fuss about Grandma's cooking. And you know how Shawn likes Korean recipes." She sighed. "What'll we do?"

There was a twinkle in her mother's eye. "Your grandma's very wise."

"Oh," said Abby.

She thought about being *very wise*. Did it mean eating dark green foods? And keeping the house perfectly clean?

Mother was grinning. "Grandma raised your father. Just think what a fine man he turned out to be."

Abby had heard her father's childhood stories. "Grandma and Grandpa had a bunch of children," she said. "Did all of them eat broccoli?"

Mother laughed out loud. "You'll have to ask Grandma about that."

Abby would ask, all right.

First thing tomorrow!

TWO

It was Friday morning. School was out for a teacher work day.

Abby brushed her sister's hair. "Hold still. I'll make a ponytail."

"Ouch, you're hurting me!" Carly wailed.

"Sorry. I'll be more careful," Abby promised. She tried to keep her mind on Carly's wavy blond hair. It was so pretty.

She tried *not* to think about the long weekend.

"When's Grandma coming?" asked Carly.

"Right after breakfast," Abby replied.

"She won't make that horrible dish, will she?" Carly asked.

"Which one?" Abby laughed. "They're *all* icky, aren't they?"

Carly pinched her nose. "What if we die from Grandma's cooking?" She was laughing, too.

Abby shushed her. "Don't say it so loud."

"Why?—because Mommy and Daddy might not go on their trip?" Carly's eyes spelled mischief.

"Grandma won't poison us," Abby assured her. "You know that!"

"Maybe . . . maybe not," added Carly, frowning.

"She loves us, you silly sister," Abby insisted.

Carly nodded. "I know. But she cooks terrible stuff."

Abby understood Carly's worry.

What a weekend ahead!

When Carly's ponytail was done, Abby snapped in a bow. "Now you're ready for our prissy grandma."

Carly looked in the dresser mirror. "Goody!" She touched her hair and the bow. Then she turned toward Abby. "Why didn't Mommy ask Granny Mae to come?"

Abby smiled. "I think you know why."

Carly wrinkled up her nose. "I do?"

Abby leaned down. She whispered in her sister's ear. "Granny Mae is crazy for sweets. She only has eyes for junk food and goodies."

"*That's* not why!" Carly insisted. "It can't be!"

"Ask Mom," Abby said. "You'll find out."

Carly shook her head. "*You* ask."

"I don't have to. I know I'm right," Abby said.

Carly tossed her head. Her ponytail brushed against her cheek. "Okay, I'll see

15

for myself." She dashed out of the bedroom.

Abby sat on the bed and sighed.

When would her sister ever believe her?

★ ★ ★

Abby helped Dad carry the suitcases to the car.

Her parents kissed her good-bye.

They kissed and hugged Carly, Shawn, and Jimmy, too.

Dad's face was serious. "Please obey your grandmother." He looked at each of them.

"We will," Abby said. She glanced at Carly. "Won't we?"

Carly was trying to keep from smiling. Abby could tell by her sister's flat lips. A giggle might burst out any minute!

Jimmy was whispering to Shawn in Korean.

Abby recognized several words.

Jimmy was telling Shawn something about broccoli.

Abby listened more carefully.

Oh no! she thought. Shawn was telling Jimmy not to eat the broccoli!

Dad caught Abby's eye. He must've heard, too. "Now, boys," he began. "You must eat your vegetables while we're gone."

"We *have* to?" Jimmy whined.

"Grandma will be in charge of you," Dad said.

Jimmy's eyes rolled around. "Green vegetables make little boy very sick." He was pointing to himself.

Shawn's face was droopy, too.

But the boys weren't going to fool Dad. Probably not Grandma Hunter, either.

"You'll eat whatever your grandmother makes," Mom said. Her words were firm.

Jimmy started to groan.

He held his stomach.

He pretended to be too sick to stand up.

Ker-plop-ity! He fell over and slammed onto the floor.

Then . . . Shawn and Carly fell over, too.

There were three kids on the floor, faking it good.

Abby shook her head. She felt like joining them, but she knew better. Her parents were watching.

"We're counting on you," Mother said. She was giving Abby "The Eye."

"The Eye" was nothing to fool around with. It meant important business.

"No funny stuff," Daddy warned. "We want a good report when we return."

Suddenly, Abby wished she wasn't the oldest. Why did the oldest kid have to behave the best? Always!

She guessed she knew why.

It was important to be a good example. For Carly, Shawn, and Jimmy.

"Okay, enough of this," Dad said. He looked at the wiggling threesome on the floor. He snapped his fingers. "C'mon! Up you go!"

Shawn, Carly, and Jimmy were on their feet. But they were still holding their stomachs and moaning.

"Don't worry," Abby told her parents. "I'll make sure everyone obeys Grandma." She glanced at her sister and brothers. "*All* weekend!"

"Since when is Abby the boss?" Carly said, making a face.

Mother and Daddy set her straight. "Abby's the oldest. She's going to help Grandma," Dad said. "End of story."

Carly made another face. A pickle face!

What a weekend, thought Abby. *What a wacky weekend!*

THREE

Grandma Hunter arrived in a yellow taxi cab.

She stepped out, wearing her pink Sunday dress. And a pretty apron. A single strand of pearls hung around her neck. And there were earrings to match.

"Let me look at you, children."

Smack! She planted a kiss on each face.

Jimmy turned around. When no one was looking, he wiped off the kiss.

Abby saw him do it. She frowned hard at him.

Jimmy shot daggers with his eyes.

But Mother and Daddy didn't notice. They were smiling, almost too pleased. Especially Mother.

Grandma Hunter greeted Mother and Daddy. "My grandchildren and I are going to have a splendid time." She glanced at Abby and the others. "Aren't we, children?"

Suddenly, Grandma wanted to hug again, starting with the youngest.

Little Jimmy got squeezed almost to nothing.

Carly and Shawn were next.

And last, Abby.

Grandma's big, chubby arms pressed in around her. "My, my, you've grown," said Grandma.

Abby was pleased about that. She was glad she was getting taller. The oldest kid should be the tallest kid.

Double dabble good!

Stepping back, Grandma smiled

sweetly. "I have the most delicious recipe for supper," she announced. "It's a surprise."

Abby shuddered. *Not tonight,* she thought. *Not the very first night.*

Then she caught her mother's eyes. Her parents had asked the kids to obey. They were expected to be polite. They must eat exactly what their grandmother cooked.

Yikes!

Abby was a jitterbox again.

★ ★ ★

Abby led Grandma to the guest room. "Here's where you'll sleep," she said.

Silently, Abby waited.

At once, Grandma began to inspect! She ran her fingers over the dresser. And over the top of the mirror. She looked under the bed and behind the nightstand.

Abby was glad she had cleaned so carefully.

At last, Grandma sat down. Her eyes discovered the flowers. "How very pretty," she said with a sigh.

Abby grinned. "The flowers were Mother's idea. But *I* cleaned your room."

Grandma was nodding. "Abby, you're an excellent housekeeper."

"Thanks." She stayed in the room. Her grandma might need some help unpacking.

Then Abby noticed a giant shopping bag. It was bursting with strange objects. Especially something round and silver.

Gulp!

The vegetable steamer!

Abby had seen the silver thingamabob before. It had come with Grandma the *last* time!

She thought of falling on the floor. She thought of holding her stomach. But Abby was the oldest. She *had* to behave. Dad and Mother would be unhappy if she didn't.

Abby didn't dare gag. She didn't dare faint on the floor. But she *did* take a deep breath. She'd have to eat steamed vegetables. Tonight!

"Grandma?" she said softly. "What's for supper?"

"Just you wait and see," Grandma said. Her eyebrows flew up over her big blue eyes. She seemed terribly excited.

Abby got her hopes up. Maybe tonight's supper wouldn't include broccoli, after all. Maybe . . .

She crossed her fingers. She didn't hope to die, though. That came easily with eating yucky vegetables!

"Did you feed Daddy broccoli when he was little?" Abby asked.

A smile swept over Grandma's face. "Ah, broccoli," she whispered. "Doesn't it have a nice ring to it?"

Abby listened. She didn't hear anything. "What ring?"

Grandma waved her hand. "Oh, never

mind that," she said. "It's the taste that counts."

"The taste?" Abby wanted to choke. How could Grandma think such a thing?

Grandma held up the vegetable steamer. "Do you have any idea about this marvelous thing?" She stared at it, admiring it. Like it was a treasure or something.

Abby tried not to frown . . . or cry. "Did my father eat broccoli when he was little? Did his brothers and sisters?"

"Is the sky blue?" Grandma Hunter replied. She touched the flowers in the vase. "Are these daisies yellow?"

Abby didn't get it. Why was her grandma asking questions right back?

Of course the sky was blue. And the flowers were yellow. Anybody could see that!

Grandma folded her hands in her lap. "Well, Abby?"

All of a sudden, she understood.

Grandma was trying to say that her children *did* like broccoli.

"They ate many kinds of vegetables," Grandma added. "Back in those days, children weren't so picky."

"So everyone ate broccoli in the olden days?" asked Abby.

Grandma laughed. "My dear girl. I don't think you understood a word I said."

Just then Abby was wrapped into a big hug.

"I love you anyway," Grandma said with a grin.

After that, Abby decided something. She would try to forget the broccoli question.

She would try *very* hard!

FOUR

"Eeyew, gross," Jimmy said at supper. He was staring at Grandma's vegetable surprise.

Abby felt jittery. Her little brother had zero manners. None!

The dark green vegetable was smothered in cheese sauce. But the green yuck poked through anyway.

Grandma's big surprise was a broccoli casserole!

Abby didn't know what to do. Should she kick Jimmy under the table? Should she give him "The Eye"?

She frowned hard at her brother. She hoped he might look her way.

But he didn't.

Jimmy kept it up. "AAAUUUGH!" he hollered. "I hate broccoli!"

Shawn's eyes popped wide.

Carly's mouth dropped open.

But Jimmy was just warming up. "Grandma not love little boy from Korea," he wailed. "Not . . . not . . . not!"

Grandma Hunter was on her feet. She hurried over to Jimmy and touched his forehead. "Are you sick, child?" she asked.

"Very sick," he cried. "Jimmy very, very sick boy."

It sounded like *velly, velly*.

Abby almost burst out laughing.

Carly and Shawn had trouble keeping a straight face, too. Abby had never seen Jimmy carry on like this.

Well . . . she had. Once before.

It was the night of Jimmy's first bath. He squealed and yelled. She thought he'd

never stop. So Abby had gone to look for her old plastic duck. When she found it, she gave it to Jimmy. He stopped crying. Just like that.

Now Abby picked up her fork. She tried to ignore her loud-mouthed little brother. It wasn't easy.

He fussed. Louder and louder.

Shawn hollered something to him in Korean. But that made things even worse.

Jimmy pushed away from the table. He looked terribly white. He was holding his stomach. Like before Dad and Mother left for the weekend.

Only *this* time he looked sick. For real.

Grandma began to fan him with her napkin. "Oh, dear boy," she said. "Let's get you to the washroom."

Jimmy was nodding his head. "Yes, hurry, hurry."

Abby couldn't believe it. Jimmy had made himself sick.

After Grandma left with Jimmy, Abby had a funny feeling.

Both Shawn and Carly were looking at her.

"What're you two staring at?" she asked.

"You're the oldest," Carly piped up. "Why didn't you do something?"

"About Jimmy?" asked Abby.

Shawn's eyes were big. "Jimmy not really sick, is he?"

Abby didn't know. "He might be faking. I'm not sure."

Shawn frowned at the broccoli. Then he stuck his finger down his throat.

"Sick," Carly said. "Really disgusting!"

Shawn ran for the washroom, gagging.

Abby shook her head.

"Do something," Carly pleaded.

"Like what?" Abby said.

Carly began to giggle. "Pour some sugar on the broccoli."

"Good thinking," Abby said.

She reached for the sugar bowl.

FIVE

Supper took forever.

Abby wondered about Jimmy and Shawn. What was happening? Were they really sick?

She drank her milk and cut her meat. She mixed bites of broccoli with mashed potatoes.

At last, Jimmy and Shawn returned to the table.

Grandma came, too. She looked worn out.

"Oooh-aaagh," Jimmy was still groaning a lot.

Grandma sat down and sighed. She sipped her coffee.

Just then Jimmy sneaked a smile at Shawn.

Now Abby knew her brothers were faking. But she kept eating her broccoli. So did Carly.

Grandma Hunter reached for the casserole dish. Next, she put a piece of meat and some potatoes on her plate.

Abby wondered if Grandma would notice how sugary the broccoli tasted. "The supper's very good," she spoke up.

"Yes, the broccoli's nice and *sweet*," Carly said.

Jimmy sat up. His eyes were wide. "Sweet? Like candy?"

"Sure, have a taste," Abby said. "You'll see."

Grandma's eyes popped wide. But she was silent.

Jimmy took one serving spoonful. "Only one little bite," he said.

Abby held her breath. Would he like it?

Jimmy tasted the vegetable. He chewed and swallowed. "Mm-m, good," he said, rubbing his tummy. "Grandma put sugar in broccoli."

"Did you say *sugar*?" Shawn said and dished up a BIG serving.

Jimmy cleaned his plate and asked for more.

But Grandma Hunter didn't say a word.

Neither did Abby.

★ ★ ★

After supper, Abby helped Grandma clean up.

Jimmy hurried past them with his hands in his pocket. He headed for the back door.

Why's he acting so strange? Abby wondered.

She went to the window and looked

out. Jimmy was feeding the ducks, Quacker and Jack.

Grandma came and peeked out the window, too. "Everyone seemed to enjoy my broccoli dish," she said. "I'll have to chop up some and put it in the scrambled eggs."

"Tomorrow for breakfast?" Abby asked. She hoped not.

"It's quite delicious," said Grandma. "It's tasty, even with *no* sugar added."

Abby's heart sank. Grandma knew what she'd done.

But besides that, Jimmy and Shawn would *never* eat eggs with broccoli. Not in a hundred years!

"What about some pancakes instead?" Abby asked.

Would Grandma take the hint?

"Well, that settles it. I'll make pancakes *and* eggs," Grandma said with a curious grin.

Abby could see it now. Nobody would eat the eggs. Not one bite. But the pancakes would disappear in a flash.

Maybe Grandma would finally get the hint. Maybe she'd forget about broccoli!

Grandma dried her hands on her apron. She turned away from the window.

Abby kept watching Jimmy. He was outside in the duck pen, feeding the ducks something dark and green.

Is that what I think it is? she wondered.

"Excuse me, Grandma," Abby said. "I'll be right back."

She darted out the kitchen door. She ran across the backyard to the duck pen. She stared at the green stuff in Jimmy's hand. "That's gross," Abby said. "What is it?"

Jimmy blinked his eyes fast. "I . . . I feed ducks leftovers." He stared down at the broccoli.

"But I thought you ate it," she said. She gave him "The Eye."

Jimmy shook his head. "Very sorry, but I not eat *all* of it."

"But you said it was sweet, like candy," Abby insisted. "You tricked us. Especially Grandma."

"Sugar not work with broccoli and cheese." He kept offering the smashed-up broccoli to the ducks.

"I thought sugar might change the taste," she said. "I promised Daddy we'd obey Grandma. *All* weekend. I was trying to help."

Jimmy talked Korean to the ducks. But it was no use. They weren't interested in leftovers. With or without sugar.

This weekend was going to be the worst ever!

Just then . . .

AH-OO-GAH! Abby heard a familiar sound. It was Granny Mae's silly car horn.

What's she *doing here?* Abby wondered.

Jimmy wiped his hands on his pants. He came running into the house. "This Sunday . . . Grandparents Day!" he hollered.

"Are you sure?" Abby asked.

Jimmy grinned. "That why Granny Mae come. She come for Grandparents Day," he said. "I see holiday on calendar."

"Granny Mae doesn't pay attention to that stuff," Abby said.

"We see about that," said Jimmy.

Abby felt funny. Why *had* Granny Mae come?

SIX

Granny Mae rushed into the house. She was wearing her favorite blue jeans and a bright T-shirt. "Hi, ya, kids," she announced.

"What are *you* doing here!" Carly squealed with delight.

Grandma Hunter gasped. "Carly, dear, that's not a polite thing to say to Granny Mae."

"Sorry, Granny," Carly said.

But Granny Mae didn't seem to mind. She was carrying a curious big bag. "I brought surprises for my grandkiddos," she said.

Shawn spied the bag of sweets. "Hi, Granny Mae," he said, grinning.

Abby was thrilled to see her, too.

"There's my Abbykins," said Granny Mae, reaching for a hug.

"Grandparents Day is this Sunday. Did you know that?" Abby asked her.

"I had no idea." Granny Mae shook her head. Her earrings dangled. Her bracelet jangled.

"Happy Grandparents Day!" shouted Carly.

"I see it first on calendar," Jimmy said. He wiped his hands on his pants.

"Come here, little pipsqueak darlin'," said Granny Mae. She wrapped her long, thin arms around Jimmy.

Jimmy giggled into the hug.

Abby crossed her fingers. She hoped Grandma Hunter wouldn't notice the broccoli stains.

Grandma pushed up her glasses. "How are you, Granny Mae?"

"I'm terrific, now that I'm here," Granny Mae replied.

The two grandmas hugged. But not for long.

"Is everything cool?" Granny Mae asked Grandma Hunter.

Grandma Hunter nodded with a little laugh. "We're getting along fine."

"Well, I thought I'd come over and help out," Granny Mae said. She looked at the kids. "Four kiddos can be a real handful."

"Can you stay all weekend?" asked Carly. "Then we'll have *two* grandmas in charge of us."

Abby knew what Carly was up to. Sure as anything. Maybe Granny Mae could save them from more broccoli.

Grandma Hunter smoothed her apron. Again and again. She did that when she was upset.

Abby wondered what Grandma

Hunter would think of Granny Mae staying.

But Granny Mae didn't think twice. "Sure, I'll stay."

Carly and Shawn hugged Granny Mae.

Abby sneaked Jimmy off to the washroom. She locked the door. "Let's see that yucky pant leg of yours," she said.

Jimmy fussed and whined. "Who cares about broccoli spots!"

Abby ignored his complaining. "We have to get it out."

Scrub-a-dub-a-dub!

Abby rubbed and rubbed. She used plenty of soap. She rinsed with hot water. Next, cold water.

Then she started all over again with soap. But she couldn't get the broccoli mark off.

"Look!" Jimmy said. "Sister make spot grow!"

It was true. The rubbing and scrubbing had made the green mark spread.

"You'll just have to change clothes," Abby said. "It's the only way."

Jimmy's tongue stuck out at her. "I not obey sister," he said. "You not make me!"

Abby sat on the edge of the bathtub. "Don't you remember what Dad said? I'm supposed to help Grandma."

Jimmy smirked. "Grandma not need your help. *Granny Mae* help Grandma now." He darted for the door.

"Hey, you can't go out like that again," Abby said. "Don't you understand?" She tried to explain. "If Grandma Hunter sees those smudges, she'll know you didn't eat all your broccoli."

"But Jimmy was sick!" he said.

"You faked it. You fooled Grandma . . . *all* of us. You hid the broccoli in your pocket," she said.

Jimmy nodded his head. "I not know what to do."

"Just *please* change your clothes," she

47

begged. "And wash your dirty hands."

Jimmy looked down at his hands and the ugly green spots on his pants. "Okay. Jimmy obey sister," he said.

It's about time! thought Abby.

She dashed down the hall to see Granny Mae.

SEVEN

"Let's celebrate!" laughed Granny Mae. She and Carly were dancing around.

"We'll eat cake and cookies and candy," said Carly.

Grandma Hunter crossed her arms. "I don't agree with all those sweets," she said. "We *did* just have supper."

Granny Mae wrinkled her nose. "Well, if the kids just ate, then it's time for dessert."

"Hoo-ray!" cheered Carly.

Abby glanced at Shawn. She felt like a total jitterbox.

Then Shawn joined Carly in a jig with Granny Mae.

"Excuse me!" Grandma Hunter made an attempt to be heard. "I'm quite certain the children are NOT hungry. And too many sweets aren't good."

Rats! thought Abby. She wanted to party!

Before Grandma Hunter could say more, Granny Mae opened her bag of sweets.

Carly and Shawn peeked inside. "Goody!" said Carly.

"Candy sticks and candy bars," said Shawn. "Yummies for my tummy."

Just then Jimmy appeared in the hallway. He'd changed jeans and washed his hands. Now he spied the sweets. "I want chocolate!" he shouted.

"No shouting indoors, please," Grandma Hunter warned.

"Sorry," Jimmy said. But he hurried over to get his candy from Granny Mae.

Abby took her time choosing a chocolate bar. Carefully, she unwrapped the
paper and bit into it. Any other day, it
would have tasted great. Today, she was
too upset to enjoy it.

"Let's sit at the table," Grandma
Hunter suggested.

The kids headed for the kitchen.

"Let's relax in the family room,"
Granny Mae said.

The kids turned toward the family
room.

"No . . . no," said Grandma Hunter.
"We don't want to soil the nice furniture."

Abby turned back to the kitchen.

"We'll be careful," Carly said.

"We not make mess," Jimmy said. But
his mouth was already dribbling pink goo.

Abby turned back toward the family
room.

"I think we better play it safe,"
Grandma Hunter said. She waved for the
kids to go into the kitchen.

51

Granny Mae nodded and followed.

By now Abby felt dizzy.

This way. That way.

Which way?

After all, Dad had said, *"Obey your grandmother."*

The problem was, he didn't say which one!

It was like a game where no one wins.

A granny game. No fun!

EIGHT

It was getting late. Bedtime at the Hunter house.

But Granny Mae said they could stay up.

And Grandma Hunter said to get ready for bed.

Carly and Jimmy obeyed Granny Mae and stayed up.

Abby and Shawn obeyed Grandma Hunter and headed for bed. Back and forth. This and that.

Who should they obey?

Eating broccoli is better than this! thought Abby.

She brushed her teeth and dressed for bed.

Grandma Hunter came to tuck her in. So did Granny Mae.

"Ready to say your prayers?" asked Grandma Hunter.

Abby knelt beside Grandma Hunter. "I'm ready."

"Why don't we *sing* your prayers?" Granny Mae suggested.

Grandma Hunter's head jerked up. "Whoever heard of that?"

"Why not?" Granny Mae said. "We'll join hands and sing in a circle."

Abby didn't know what to do. She could see that Grandma Hunter was unhappy. In fact, Grandma looked terribly tired. Too tired to stand, hold hands, and sing "Now I Lay Me . . ."

But she surprised Abby and went along with it.

When the prayer was sung, Abby crawled into bed.

"Sleep tight, honey," said Grandma Hunter.

"Don't let the bed bugs bite," said Granny Mae. "If they bite, squeeze 'em tight. Then they won't bite another night."

Grandma Hunter left the room.

But Granny Mae stayed. "Are you sure you're tired, Abbykins?" she asked.

"I better go to bed," Abby told her.

"You could sleep in tomorrow. It's Saturday, you know."

"I know," Abby said. "It's just . . ."

"Just what?"

Abby paused. "I wake up real early. Mother calls me an early bird."

"That's cool," said Granny Mae. "We need early birds to catch worms. Good night, kiddo."

"See you in the morning." Abby snuggled down into bed.

★ ★ ★

Abby's dreams were all mixed up.

Granny Mae baked chocolate cake with candy sprinkles for breakfast.

Grandma Hunter cut up celery and carrot sticks for dessert.

"Choose your favorite food," both grandmothers said in the dream.

First, Abby stared at the gooey cake. Then she looked at the raw vegetables. "I like both kinds of food," she said. "Both grandmas, too."

She didn't want to hurt their feelings. What should she decide?

She took a handful of carrots and celery. And she poked them into the chocolate icing on the cake.

"Double dabble good," she said.

But she said it so loud, she woke herself up!

Abby sat up in bed. She rubbed her eyes.

The moon smiled through the window. But Abby frowned back.

NINE

It was Saturday morning.

Abby opened one eye. She stared at the ceiling. She listened.

The house was quiet, except for a whirring sound.

Grandma Hunter must be up, cooking. Probably pancakes!

Abby leaped out of bed. She remembered what Granny Mae had said: *"The early bird catches the worm."*

And . . . the early bird gets the first pancake!

She slipped into her bathrobe and hurried to the kitchen.

Shawn had beat her to it. He was already sitting at the table. Another early bird.

"Good morning, Abby," said Grandma Hunter.

"Good morning," replied Abby. "How'd you sleep?"

Before she could answer, Granny Mae was standing in the doorway. She had a curious grin on her face. "She slept the way everyone does . . . by lying down and blacking out." Then she burst out laughing.

Abby couldn't help it. She laughed, too.

But Grandma Hunter was NOT laughing. She faced the window and smoothed her apron.

She's upset again, thought Abby.

She sat at the table, next to Shawn. "What's for breakfast?" she asked.

Shawn whispered, "Dry potato cakes with *no* syrup."

"Anything else?" asked Abby, worried.

"Oatmeal with leftover broccoli." His face scrunched up like a prune.

"You're kidding, right?" Abby said.

Shawn shook his head sadly. "I say the truth."

Just then Granny Mae went to the fridge. She pulled out a chocolate cake.

Abby gasped. It was the same one from her dream. Or nightmare. She couldn't decide which.

Granny placed the cake right in front of Abby's nose.

Shawn's eyes blinked fast. "Dessert for breakfast?" he said.

"Eat it whenever you wish," Granny Mae said.

Abby couldn't believe her ears. What would her parents say? But . . . wait! Dad had said to *Obey your grandmother.*

Granny Mae was her grandmother. So maybe it was okay to eat chocolate cake for breakfast!

Grandma Hunter brought over a platter of potato cakes. They were made from mashed potatoes. Last night's leftovers! *Ick!*

Next, Grandma brought over a huge bowl of oatmeal. Abby could see the teeny-tiny bits of broccoli. There was no hiding them!

It was an easy choice.

Abby had a piece of chocolate cake with her dry pancakes.

Shawn had one dry pancake with his moist cake.

Abby glanced at Shawn, then at Grandma Hunter. "I think we better wake up Carly and Jimmy."

The grandmothers agreed about that. It was a first!

Abby, Shawn, and the grandmothers marched down the hall. "Good morning to you, good morning to you . . ." Granny Mae sang as they went.

"The early bird catches the worm," chanted Abby.

"Better not be any worms in my chocolate cake," replied Granny Mae.

Shawn was laughing hard. "Wake up, Jimmy! Wake up, Carly!" he called.

Carly was too sleepy to wake up. "I stayed up too late," she said and rolled over.

Jimmy said the same thing.

Grandma Hunter shook her head. She wouldn't have allowed Jimmy and Carly to stay up so late. Her eyebrows rose and stayed high on her forehead.

"I guess I'll have to eat the chocolate cake by myself," Granny Mae announced. She said it loud enough for Carly to hear.

That got them up. Jimmy first, then Carly.

"Are we really having dessert for breakfast?" Carly asked. She rubbed her eyes awake. She must've thought she was dreaming.

Jimmy ran to the kitchen. "Sugar very good for you," he hollered. "Just like a vitamin!"

Grandma Hunter's lips were tight. She offered bananas and orange juice. And the awful oatmeal.

Granny Mae held up the gooey cake.

Carly and Jimmy were grinning. They chose the cake!

Grandma Hunter's face turned red. "Remember to say grace," she said.

Probably so we won't die, Abby thought.

"We could sing our prayer," Granny Mae said with a smile.

"Mommy says *not* to sing at the table," Carly piped up.

"Carly's right," Abby said.

"Better *say* prayer," Shawn spoke up.

"And hurry . . . hurry," said Jimmy, staring at the cake.

Abby blessed the food. And thanked God for *both* her grandmothers.

"Dig in!" Granny Mae said.

"Be neat," said Grandma Hunter.

Abby spread her napkin on her lap. She cut her slice of cake and placed it on top of her dry pancake. But she didn't take any oatmeal with green broccoli dots. Nope!

Snow White, the dog, wandered over to the table. She sniffed around Abby's plate.

"Are you hungry?" Abby whispered. She lifted up the bowl of oatmeal.

Snow White took one whiff and backed away.

"The dog doesn't know what's good," said Grandma Hunter.

Abby bit her tongue. She knew better than to say otherwise.

"Ducks not like broccoli, either," Jimmy blurted.

Grandma Hunter's face turned purple. Her hands shook. "Ducks? Who's feeding my beautiful broccoli to the ducks?" she asked.

Jimmy slumped down in his chair. "Oops," he whispered.

Yikes! thought Abby.

TEN

Breakfast was over.

Abby and Shawn helped Grandma Hunter clean the kitchen.

Carly and Jimmy helped Granny Mae make the beds.

Abby could hear Granny Mae whistling in the bedrooms. And there were giggles, too. Lots of them.

Carefully, Abby rinsed the plates. She handed them to Shawn. He put them in the dishwasher.

It was so quiet. No one was whistling in

the kitchen. Not Shawn. Not Abby. And not Grandma Hunter.

Abby turned on the radio. It was time for Saturday morning jazz, the Dixieland kind. Squealing clarinets and a romping piano!

She jigged around the table. She waved the dish towel in the air. Shawn joined in, too.

But Grandma Hunter shuffled past them, out of the room.

"Grandma is very upset," Shawn whispered.

Abby nodded. "I know."

"At least we're safe from broccoli," said Shawn, laughing.

"Maybe," replied Abby.

But broccoli didn't matter right now.

★　★　★

Abby went looking for Granny Mae. She found her downstairs in the family room. "I think we have a problem," Abby told her. "It's about Grandma Hunter."

Granny Mae's eyes popped wide. "What's wrong?"

Abby tried to explain. "Grandma Hunter likes things . . . uh, just so." She paused.

Granny chuckled. "That's nothing new. Everyone knows Grandma Hunter's fussy that way."

"But she's *unhappy*," Abby insisted. "I think we hurt her feelings."

"Oh dear," Granny Mae said. "I was afraid of that. I suppose I should've stayed home."

"No, Granny, we're glad you came. After all, it's Grandparents Day tomorrow," Abby said. "But how can we make Grandma cheerful again?"

Granny Mae scratched her head. "Let's see. . . ." She thought and thought.

Then she jumped up off the sofa. "You just leave that to me, Abbykins." And she marched down the hall and knocked on the guest room door.

Abby gulped. *What have I done?*

★ ★ ★

Two grandmas were locked away in the guest room.

Abby watched the kitchen clock.

The minutes ticked by.

She and Carly, Jimmy, and Shawn sat around the table. They were silent. They looked back and forth at one another.

"What if Granny Mae goes home?" Carly worried.

Abby shrugged. "She's up to something. I know that much."

Jimmy rolled his eyes. "I like fun Granny. She very cool."

Shawn poked his brother. "And I like prissy Grandma. She give great hugs."

Abby heard several footsteps. "Shh! Someone's coming!"

The kids sat up straight . . . waiting.

Then Granny Mae and Grandma Hunter strolled into the kitchen. Their arms were linked together!

Abby's mouth dropped open. *What's going on?* she wondered.

"Everything's cool, kiddos," Granny Mae announced. "Grandma Hunter and I have come to an agreement."

Grandma Hunter's eyes were shining. "You dear children," she said. "You've been all mixed up this weekend. One strict grandma and one happy-go-lucky granny—both of us trying to take good care of you."

Granny Mae agreed. "You kiddos have been trying to please both of us. That's too much to ask."

Abby listened. *What's the agreement?* she wondered.

Grandma Hunter continued. "There's a time for dessert . . ."

"And there's a time for broccoli," added Granny Mae.

"Both are important," the grandmas said together.

"There's a time to party," said Grandma Hunter.

"And there's a time to work," Granny Mae said. "And something else. We've agreed to be a team . . . Grandma and I."

"And," said Grandma Hunter, "we've agreed to a party!" She was grinning.

The Hunter kids cheered. "Hoo-ray!"

"When's the party?" Carly asked.

"Tomorrow, right after church," said Granny Mae.

"For Grandparents Day?" Jimmy asked, wide-eyed.

"Double dabble good idea!" shouted Abby.

Grandma Hunter sat at the table. "Let's plan a big dinner party," she said. "What would you like to eat?"

Anything but broccoli, thought Abby. But she was polite. "We all like pasta," she suggested.

Grandma's eyes sparkled. "We'll have a spaghetti feast."

"With meat sauce?" Carly asked.

"Oh, certainly," said Grandma Hunter.

"Just *plain* meat sauce?" Abby asked.

She had to make sure no vegetables would be floating around.

Granny Mae spoke up. "We'll have vegetables on the side. But no broccoli tomorrow."

"And we'll have plenty of desserts after dinner," Grandma added.

"Can we invite Grandpa Hunter?" asked Carly.

"Of course," Grandma said. She looked at Granny Mae. "And while you're at it, invite your friends, too."

Abby gasped.

Was this for real?

"We want to meet the Cul-de-sac Kids," Grandma Hunter said. "Don't we, Granny?"

"*All* of them?" asked Abby.

Granny Mae stuck up both her thumbs. "You got it, girl. We'll have a pasta picnic in the backyard."

"Invite their grandparents, too," Grandma Hunter said.

Abby couldn't stop laughing. Her jitters were gone.

The Granny Game was the best. Nobody had to win, after all.

Double dabble terrific!

THE CUL-DE-SAC KIDS SERIES
Don't Miss #21!
MYSTERY MUTT

Stacy Henry makes some New Year's goals based on the Fruit of the Spirit. One by one, the Cul-de-sac Kids choose a "fruit." All except Jason Birchall, who thinks the idea is silly.

Then someone leaves a shabby puppy on his doorstep. And stubborn Jason picks "gentleness" for his New Year's fruit. Stacy and Jason search for the dog's owner, with no success.

Will Stacy's mother let her keep the dirty pooch? Will Jason's? Can the Cul-de-sac Kids harvest a crop of kindness?

About the Author

Beverly Lewis remembers spending time with both grandmothers while she was growing up. One lived in Pennsylvania and often sang hymns as she cooked delicious casseroles. The other lived in Kansas and prayed as she baked chocolate chip cookies mixed with love.

Both grandmothers made broccoli and chocolate cake. They each gave sweet hugs and kisses. "Neither one was just like the other," says Beverly. "But they both loved Jesus and prayed that I would grow to love Him, too!"

If you like humor and mystery, collect *all* the CUL-DE-SAC KIDS books. You won't be sorry!

Go for the Gold
WITH BEVERLY LEWIS!

With her fast-paced GIRLS ONLY series, Beverly Lewis opens the door to the world of Olympic sports like gymnastics, figure skating, skiing, and more. Written just for girls like you in Beverly's unique heart-to-heart style, the GIRLS ONLY series is about courage, perseverance, friendship, and standing up for what you know is right.

Set among a group of girls determined to remain friends even as they try to balance practice, school, and competition, each GIRLS ONLY book will bring you deeper into their hearts and dreams. Join them and grow in both your faith and your love of sports!

1. *Dreams on Ice*
2. *Only the Best*
3. *A Perfect Match*
4. *Reach for the Stars*
5. *Follow the Dream*
6. *Better Than Best*
7. *Photo Perfect*
8. *Star Status*

◊BETHANYHOUSE

Source Code: BOBHPA